Used under license by Penguin Young Readers Group
Published in Great Britain by Ladybird Books Ltd, 2006
80 Strand London WC2R 0RL
A Penguin Company

1 3 5 7 9 10 8 6 4 2

Printed in China

LADYBIRD and the device of a ladybird
are trademarks of Ladybird Books Ltd

Zada's Birthday Jeans

It's Zada's birthday! Her friends are helping her find the perfect outfit for her birthday party.

"These jeans used to be my favourites," said Zada, holding them up, "but now they look so boring."
"You're the birthday girl," said Ailani, "so you have to look fabulous!"
"This mini skirt is sweet," suggested Talia.
Zada held up the skirt, then smiled.

"Well girls, we've finally found my birthday outfit!" said Zada as she modelled the skirt.

"It took us long enough!" exclaimed Nazalia, pointing to the mountain of clothes on the bed. The girls laughed.

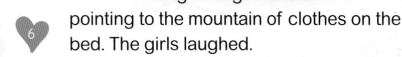

Ailani picked up Zada's old jeans. "Can I borrow these?" she asked Zada.
"Keep them," answered Zada. "I'm tired of them."
"Great!" said Ailani.

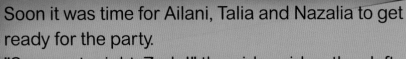

Soon it was time for Ailani, Talia and Nazalia to get
ready for the party.
"See you tonight, Zada!" the girls said as they left.

As they walked home, the girls talked about Zada's birthday gift.

"Let's give Zada her old jeans as a present!" said Ailani.

"No way, Ailani!" said Nazalia. "We've got to think of something better than that."

"We can make her old jeans into cool new jeans!" explained Ailani. "Let's all gather pretty decorations we could use to make them look awesome." Later, they met up to show what they'd found.

"Since Zada's nickname is 'Sweetheart'," said Talia, "I brought this gorgeous pink velvet heart."

"And these pink beads will look cool around the pockets," said Nazalia.

The three friends happily got to work on
Zada's birthday gift.

"Zada isn't going to recognise these jeans when we're finished!" said Ailani.
"This is such a great idea!" said Talia.
Ailani practised her design on paper, then painted a cute pattern on the jeans using special fabric paint. Talia sewed the heart onto one leg of the jeans.

Suddenly the girls heard a knock on the door. Ailani opened the door. It was Zada!

"Hi!" said Zada, "Do you guys want to hang out before the party?"

"Well, um…we're pretty busy right now," said Ailani. "Sorry."

"Zada looked so disappointed," said Ailani.
"She thinks her best friends don't want to
spend time with her on her birthday," said
Nazalia.

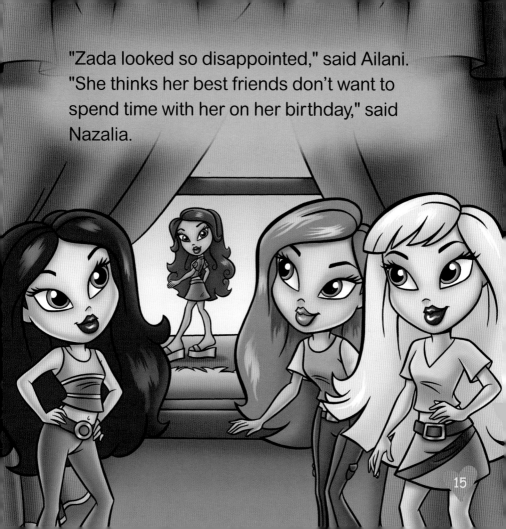

The girls worked hard to finish the jeans so they could hurry over to Zada's house and keep her company.

"I've got the perfect finishing touch!" said Ailani.
"Let's write Zada's name in tiny stars."
"Fantastic!" said Nazalia.
As Nazalia and Talia wrapped up the present, Ailani wrote a birthday card to Zada.

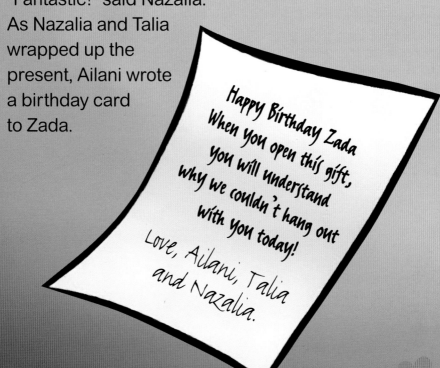

Happy Birthday Zada
When you open this gift,
you will understand
why we couldn't hang out
with you today!

Love, Ailani, Talia
and Nazalia.

"Wow!" cried Zada as she opened their gift and
card. "My old jeans! They look amazing!"

 "So now do you understand why we couldn't
hang out today?" asked Ailiani.

"I sure do – you weren't ignoring me, you were making my gift," exclaimed Zada. "My old jeans are fantastic, and so are my friends!"
As her girls gathered around her for a birthday hug, Zada said, "This is the best birthday ever!"